MASTER OF THE BEASTS

VOLTREX
THE TWO-HEADED
OCTOPUS

With special thanks to Allan Frewin Jones

To Bodhi Churchill

www.beastquest.co.uk

ORCHARD BOOKS
338 Euston Road, London NW1 3BH
Orchard Books Australia
Level 17/207 Kent St, Sydney, NSW 2000

A Paperback Original
First published in Great Britain in 2012

Beast Quest is a registered trademark of Beast Quest Limited
Series created by Beast Quest Limited, London

Text © Beast Quest Limited 2012
Inside illustrations by Pulsar Estudio (Beehive Illustration)
Cover by Steve Sims © Orchard Books 2012

ISBN 978 1 40831 521 7

1 3 5 7 9 10 8 6 4 2

Printed and bound by CPI Group (UK) Ltd, Croydon, CR0 4YY

The paper and board used in this paperback are natural recyclable
products made from wood grown in sustainable forests. The
manufacturing processes conform to the environmental regulations of
the country of origin.

Orchard Books is a division of Hachette Children's Books,
an Hachette UK company

www.hachette.co.uk

VOLTREX
THE TWO-HEADED
OCTOPUS

BY ADAM BLADE

ORCHARD

THE ICY F

THE

THE NORTHERN
MOUNTAINS

WESTERN OCEAN

THE FOREST
OF FEAR

TH

7651432

So... You still wish to follow Tom on his Beast Quest.

Turn back now. A great evil lurks beneath Avantia's earth, waiting to arise and conquer the kingdom with violence and rage. Six Beasts with the hearts of Ancient Warriors, at the mercy of the Evil Wizard, Malvel, who I fear has reached the height of his powers.

War awaits us all.

I beg you, again, close this book and turn away. Evil will rise. Darkness will fall.

Your friend,
Wizard Aduro

PROLOGUE

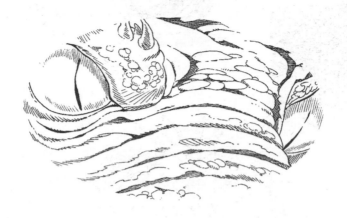

Arianna sat back on her stool, a
stick of charcoal in one hand as she
surveyed the sandy shoreline towards
the Western Ocean.

She gazed at the beautiful scenery,
then turned back to her easel and
parchment. She had drawn the
outline of a grassy dune above
the beach. Smiling to herself, she
sketched a few more details – the
foaming surf, the deep ripple of the
incoming waves, a few puffs of cloud

dancing across the sky.

"There's nothing I love more than to create a picture right here on the seashore," she murmured to herself.

Although the sea in front of her was empty, Arianna's imagination took over and she began to sketch a ship. She gave it tall masts and sails that bulged in the wind.

She added a name to the curving prow: *The Gorgon Voyager*.

"There, and now you're real – to me at least," she muttered.

All her life, Arianna had heard the stories of the strange ship *The Gorgon Voyager*. She loved those old tales – of how the ship sank near the beach, hundreds of years ago. No one knew where it had come from, nor where it was going. The stories spoke of a vast fortune still held within the rotting timbers of the old ship's hull.

Arianna looked away from her drawing as her eye caught something in the water – a curved shape that glinted in the sunlight. She stood up, shielding her eyes from the sunlight with her hand.

She gave a gasp of surprise. The object was a steel helmet – and it was rising out of the swell. Water poured from the eye-holes as more of the figure emerged from the waves.

It was a man – a huge warrior clad in gleaming blue armour.

She sat down, her heart thundering. "It's impossible," she gasped. "He must have risen from beneath the ocean itself." With shaking hands, Arianna placed a fresh sheet of parchment on her easel and began to rapidly sketch the Blue Knight.

"Now I'll have something truly extraordinary to show my friends!"

The armoured knight strode from the surf and marched up the beach, the seawater still trickling from the joints of his armour.

She drew faster, determined to make a likeness of him before she was spotted. But the man moved more quickly than she had expected and suddenly his cold shadow loomed over her. Struck by a sudden terror, Arianna let the stick of charcoal fall from her fingers as she stared up at the awful apparition.

"Who are you?" Arianna asked, hardly able to speak through the fear that clogged her throat. "Where have you come from?"

The knight reached out a hand, knocking the easel aside and sending

it spinning to the ground. Arianna
gulped in fear. *I should have run away,*
she thought. *I've been such a fool!*

The knight bent towards her and

she saw the blueish glint of inhuman eyes from inside his helmet. Then he caught hold of her around the waist, jerking her off her feet. Arianna screamed and writhed as he tucked her beneath his arm.

The Blue Knight turned and marched silently back towards the Ocean.

Arianna could barely breathe as he carried her down the beach. She choked and fought, struggling helplessly in his vice-like grip.

"Someone help me!" she gasped. No one was there. No one heard.

Water splashed on her legs and arms. She stared down in horror. The knight was wading into the sea. Desperate, Arianna kicked and beat at him with her legs and fists. The armour bruised her knees and grazed her knuckles, but still she thrashed at him.

Then – with a rush of horror – she realized that the arm holding her was no longer hard – no longer solid. It had become soft and moist and disgusting. Something wet brushed her face. It was the tip of a tentacle, lined with pulsating suckers. She opened her mouth to scream, but the tentacle whipped around her face, covering her mouth and stifling her voice.

Water surged all around her, filled with bubbles, as she was dragged under the waves. The tentacle that covered her face moved, twisting her head around.

Through the rush and surge of the water, she found herself staring into the eyes of a monstrous two-headed

octopus. She struggled again as the
foul creature loomed closer. Clouds of
darkness blurred her sight, her lungs
cried out for air.

The last thing she saw before she

lost consciousness was the hulking prow of a huge ship on the Ocean bed. She saw its name.

The Gorgon Voyager.

CHAPTER ONE

JOURNEY INTO DARKNESS

"Fresh oats, Storm!" said Tom, tipping the grain into a trough. "Good food makes a change, doesn't it?" His horse snorted and nodded his head before tucking into the welcome food. Tom smiled at the sounds of his contented chomping. Silver the wolf lay nearby, a juicy, well-gnawed marrowbone between his paws.

Tom and his animal friends were outside the hut where Sana the medicine woman lived. Steam wafted out through the doorway. Elenna and Sana were busy inside, brewing up medicine from Tengi leaves they had gathered in a large pot that bubbled and frothed over the fire.

Elenna had already made some medicine to cure Sana's blindness. The poor woman had been unable to see since her encounter with Lustor the Acid Dart, the Evil Beast that had dwelt in the sulphurous marshes around the Stonewin volcano.

"Why is this taking so long?" Tom said, slipping Aduro's globe map from his shirt and looking at it. He balanced the orb on his palm, wincing a little as the smooth surface pressed against the injury on his hand. The red raw flesh of his palm was throbbing despite Elenna's healing herbs. The Tengi leaves had prevented Lustor's acid burns from becoming infected, but they did little for the pain. Tom had been hurt when he had attacked the Red Knight and his sword had become blazingly hot from the knight's fiery armour.

Tom felt tired and in need of a good rest – they all did – but despite the exhaustion caused by their battle with Lustor and the deadly Varkule, Tom could not relax. It was only a matter of time until they found out where their next enemy lay.

The globe's marble surface showed a map of Avantia. In the past, every time a Knight of Forton had been defeated, the globe had shown the path to the next Evil Beast. Weary as he was, Tom knew that all his exhaustion would fall away once he had a clear path to his next battle!

Elenna and Sana emerged from the hut. Portos, Sana's tame bird, fluttered around them, chirruping.

"Has anything happened yet?" Elenna asked.

"Nothing," Tom replied. "This is the most urgent Quest of all. A lot of people have been harmed – Good Beasts and innocent folk." He looked at Elenna. "We have to stop the last three knights before they do more damage."

"It's not the knights' fault," Elenna reminded him gently. "They used to be a force for good in Avantia – it's only Malvel's wicked spell that has corrupted them."

Tom nodded, his eyes narrowing in anger. When this Quest had begun, they had been told that the Evil

Wizard Malvel was trapped in his own kingdom of Gorgonia. But his imprisonment had released a powerful spell, awakening the Knights of Forton from the underground Gallery of Tombs, twisting them with his powerful spells so they became evil. Worse still, they could take on the forms of the terrible Beasts they had defeated long ago.

"While you await news of your next Quest," Sana said, interrupting Tom's thoughts, "please stay and eat some food. After all you've done, it's the least I can offer."

"We'd enjoy that, thank you," said Tom. The three of them went into the hut. "We may as well," Tom muttered to Elenna, as they followed their friend. "What choice do we have?"

Tom awoke with a start. Elenna was curled up in a chair next to him, sleeping soundly under a blanket that Sana had spread over her. The hut was full of rosy firelight, but through the door, Tom could see that it was pitch dark outside. Portos perched on a shelf, his head tucked under his wing.

"Fool!" Tom muttered to himself, getting to his feet. He drew out the globe. "I knew it!" he cried. "I should never have let myself fall asleep. Elenna! Wake up – we've been shown the path!"

Elenna stood up, rubbing her eyes. She leant over Tom's arm, blinking at the silvery route that snaked across the length of the Kingdom to the Western Ocean.

"What's written there?" she asked.

"Voltrex," Tom read. "And I know which of the Good Beasts it will attack."

"Sepron. Of course!" said Elenna.

Tom snatched up his shield. The Sea Serpent's tooth embedded in the shield was yellowed and faded – a sign that their friend was in danger.

"While we slept, one of the Knights could already have reached him!" declared Tom. "We have to leave at once. There's no time to lose."

CHAPTER TWO

A RACE TO THE SEA

Elenna scribbled a farewell note to
Sana before they slipped out into
the night.

"I can't believe I fell asleep when a
Good Beast is in danger!" Tom chided
himself as he saddled Storm and
climbed onto the horse's back. Elenna
sprang up behind him.

"Don't blame yourself," she said.
"I fell asleep, too."

"We'll have to ride like the wind to get to the Ocean in time to help," said Tom, slapping Storm's neck. "Go boy, as fast as you can!"

Silver streaked ahead, a grey shadow in the starlit night. But they had hardly begun the long journey before the wolf came to a sudden halt. He lifted his muzzle and howled.

"He's seen something," said Elenna.

Tom reined Storm in, staring ahead as a ghostly shape flickered into view beside the wolf.

"Aduro!" gasped Tom, alarmed by how haggard and weak the image of the Good Wizard looked.

"Your mission is more vital than you could ever imagine," came the Wizard's voice. "Malvel grows stronger by the hour."

"What about Sepron?" asked Tom.

"Even now, he is doing battle with one of the Knights of Forton." Aduro's eyes were haunted. "The knight has turned into a terrible Beast."

"How can we get there in time?" Tom cried, more angry with himself than ever.

"I will try and use my magic to take you to the Western Ocean," said Aduro.

The Wizard rose to his full height as he began to chant a spell. Tom could see that it was taking all of Aduro's remaining strength. He felt the air prickling, as though wasps were swarming all around him. The stars swam in the sky. Silver gave a yelp of fright and leapt towards them.

"Good luck," came Aduro's fading

voice. "The fate of Avantia is on your
shoulders."

The air howled in Tom's ears for
a second and then everything became
still. The only sound now was the
slow rhythmic wash of surf on
a beach.

Elenna gave a gasp of surprise. The
four of them were alone on a moonlit
stretch of rolling sand dunes.

A shred of cloud slipped across the face of the moon as Tom dismounted. Silver's eyes glittered. Neither of the animals seemed any the worse for their magical journey.

"What's that?" called Elenna, pointing to something diamond-shaped that lay glinting in the sand close to the lapping waves. As the water flowed over it, Tom saw it move. Were the waves nudging it or was it alive? Tom approached cautiously, drawing his sword. Climbing down from Storm's back, Elenna fitted an arrow to her bowstring.

As the moon broke free of the cloud, Tom saw a bearded man hunched in the sand close to the glistening shape. The man nodded and grinned toothlessly at them.

"You don't need to use your sword on old Santo," he cackled.

Tom lowered his blade. "What are you doing here?" he asked.

"I've lived here for years," Santo replied, "combing this beach for some sign of the mystic treasure that lies drowned with *The Gorgon Voyager*." He blinked at them and grinned again, pointing at the slick object. "And at last I've found it." He stooped and picked the diamond-shaped object up. Tom came closer, finally recognizing it as one of Sepron's hard green scales.

He turned to Elenna, his heart in his mouth. "This must have been broken off in a battle," he said.

"It's a much better treasure than this other thing," continued Santo, pulling a crumpled scrap of parchment from his tunic. "I found it this afternoon, but I don't think it comes from the ship."

Elenna stepped forwards and looked closely at the scrap of parchment. "There's an unfinished drawing on it," she told Tom. She took the parchment and smoothed it out.

Tom peered at the hastily scribbled outline of a man in full armour.

"It must be a Knight of Forton," said Tom. He looked at Santos. "May we keep this?"

But the old man had gone wandering up the beach, clutching Sepron's scale and muttering to himself. Tom gritted his teeth, racked with guilt. Had Sepron perished while he slept? He looked again at the Sea Serpent's tooth on his shield. It was turning brown at the edges, but it had not crumbled away.

"There may still be time to save him," Tom declared. He looked to and fro along the beach. "The only way to be sure of finding him is if we head out onto the ocean," he said. "And if we find Sepron, we're sure to find the knight."

"There are plenty of pieces of driftwood on the beach," said Elenna. "We could gather them and tie them with seaweed to make a raft."

Tom nodded and the two friends began gathering the driftwood and lashing them together with the tough seaweed.

Tom was in too much of a rush to find Sepron for anything more than a brief farewell to Storm and Silver. They dragged their new vessel down to the waterline, then waded into the surf, heaving the raft along with them. Hauling themselves aboard, Tom and Elenna paddled with wide pieces of wood.

Thick clouds had begun to crawl across the sky, blotting out the stars and the moon. As they cleared the last of the white surf the sky was suddenly torn apart by a fearsome crack of lightning. Thunder roared all around them and rain lashed down, splashing into their faces.

Storm whinnied with alarm from the beach and they heard Silver howling.

"Don't worry!" Tom called to the animals, determined not to show them any fear. "Everything will be all right!"

The sea rose around them, tipping their raft dangerously, spitting white

foam over them. Tom clung on as
the thunder boomed again and forks
of blinding lightning seared across
the sky.

He saw Elenna's anxious eyes in the gloom. A giant wave swelled up, rolling menacingly towards them.

"Hang on!" said Tom, clutching the edge of the raft.

CHAPTER THREE

CAST ADRIFT

The great wave slammed into the fragile raft, soaking them with spray. Tom and Elenna were on their knees, clinging to the creaking and straining strips of seaweed that held the timber craft together. The waves lifted around them like great rolling hills. At one moment they were perched perilously on a foaming wave crest, then they were plunged down into a deep swirling trough with the mountainous waves crashing all around them.

Tom's injured hand smarted at the touch of the salt water, but he hung on grimly, determined that he would not allow a storm to be the end of them.

Elenna called out through the rain. "I see something!"

Tom turned his head to follow her pointing finger.

A dark bundle was bobbing in the water. A violent flash of lightning burst above them and Tom saw a face in the water – a pale, upturned face!

"It's a person!" he howled above the hammering of the rain. "We must try to get to them!"

Tom knelt at Elenna's side, the two of them digging their paddles into the sea, trying desperately to bring the raft closer to the figure.

"Watch out!" Tom yelled as a vast black wave reared high above them. It crashed down like an avalanche but the seaweed ropes held. They emerged from the deluge on the back of the next wave and Tom saw that they were almost on top of the person.

It was a woman. Tom leant perilously far out from the little craft and grabbed at a handful of clothing. He dragged the woman closer and Elenna managed to get a grip on the hanging loops of seaweed that were tangled around her waist.

Together, heaving and straining, they pulled the woman up onto the raft. She lay on her back, her face white and her eyes closed. The coils

of seaweed around her waist trailed
to the edge of the raft and vanished
down into the water.

"Is she alive?" gasped Tom.

Elenna rested her head on the
woman's chest. "Yes," she said.
"Barely. But look." She picked

a triangle of shining green from among the seaweed. "It's another of Sepron's scales."

"He must be close by," said Tom. "Can you take this woman back to the shore, Elenna? I'm going to search under the sea. Sepron's tooth on my shield will protect me from drowning and the knight's heavy armour may slow him down under this water."

Elenna looked anxiously at him. "The tooth won't protect you from whatever Beast the knight may turn into," she said. "We should have brought the tokens.'

Tom frowned. "That's my fault," he said. "I was in such a hurry to get going that I forgot them. There's no time to go back for them now."

He drew his sword and gripped his

shield. "It will be hard to fight under the sea, but I have to stop the knight before more harm is done."

Elenna's face creased into a worried frown. "I can't let you fight alone," she said. "I won't leave you out here!"

"Someone else needs you right now," Tom said, looking at the woman lying on the raft. "Unless you get her to the shore, she might die. We can't let more innocent people suffer because of Malvel's wickedness." He crawled to the edge of the raft. "I'll see you very soon," he said. He grabbed at the hanging seaweed. "I'll cut her loose from this seaweed," he said, swinging his sword.

The weed was thick and tough, and Tom had to strike it two or three times to cut it away. He noticed that it had looped itself around his wrist in a tight knot. Tom felt the raft drift one way as the weeds tugged him the other. He was pulled off the raft with a cry.

"Tom!" he heard Elenna call.

The water swallowed him. Down and down he plunged, dragged into the inky ocean depths by the seaweed fronds and swift currents. Bubbles filled his eyes, making it hard for him to see anything as he sank deeper.

At least I can breathe, he thought.

Finally, he came to a painful, crashing halt on the rocky seabed. He lay on his front, his head spinning from the speed of his descent. He took a few moments to recover before he lifted his sword. The blade felt heavy and unwieldy in the water, but he

brought it down, slashing through
the seaweed tangles that still clung
to his wrist.

Something moved close by. He lifted
his head and saw a blue armoured
boot stamp down on the rocks a
hand's-breadth away from his face.

He looked up. A tall knight in blue

armour loomed over him in the gloom. "What are you searching for down here, boy?" The knight's words came out in a rush of bubbles. "It is only your own death that you will find!"

The knight held a mace in his gauntleted hands, and before Tom had the chance to do anything, the great arms came swinging down. The deadly club arced towards Tom's head.

CHAPTER FOUR

OCEAN BATTLE

Tom rolled aside as the mace crashed
into the rocky seabed, the vicious
weapon sending up clouds of sand
and shards of splintered stone. He
found his feet and came up with
his sword and shield at the ready.
Tom pushed off with both feet and
launched himself at the knight
through the murky waters. He
slashed with his sword, but the water

49

slowed his blow and the knight was able to step back so that only the tip struck the gleaming breastplate.

The knight lifted his arms slowly, fighting against the pressure of the deep water. He wielded the mace with the spiked ball of metal at its end. Down it came again, missing Tom by a fraction as he swam aside. Tom aimed another blow with his sword but the knight parried it easily, the force jarring Tom's arm.

Silvery fish darted away as they fought. Lobsters and other half-seen creatures scuttled from beneath their feet, throwing up plumes of sand and gravel.

Tom moved from side to side, stabbing at the Knight and beating at him with his shield, gradually driving him backwards across the ocean bed.

All the while, Tom was searching for some sign that Sepron was close by. Again and again the mighty mace swung, but Tom was as fast as an eel in the water, squirming this way and that, rising and dropping suddenly, keeping the knight off-guard as he fought to deliver a telling blow with his sword.

Why is the Knight fighting me under the sea? Tom wondered. *Why attack me down here rather than on land?*

As Tom battled the knight across the sea bed, the curved edge of something appeared in the dark water behind his opponent. At first Tom couldn't make it out – then he realized it was an ancient and barnacle-encrusted anchor, jutting up from the sand. A long rusty chain stretched up towards what looked like a huge, sheer cliff.

Tom waited for a downward blow from the mace, then swam up above the reach of the knight. He realized that the dark shape was actually the hull of a ship. Tangled fronds of seaweed hung from its portholes and timbers, fish swam between its rotting planks while crabs and other creatures scuttled in its mighty shadow.

A shiver ran down Tom's spine at the sight of the eerie wreck; he had the feeling that he knew the name of the doomed ship: *The Gorgon Voyager*.

The Blue Knight kicked off the sea bed up towards Tom, his mace poised to strike, but with a flick of his legs, Tom sped upwards out of reach. As they crested the steep side of the hull Tom planted his feet on the deck. The knight's metal feet stamped

down beside him, shaking the rotting
timbers.

"Where is Sepron?" Tom cried,
Sepron's scale allowing him to speak
despite being under the sea. His heart

beat wildly with the effort of moving through the deep water. "What have you done with him?"

The knight did not respond, but his evil blue eyes gleamed through the visor. He surged forwards, bringing his mace down. Tom dodged aside and the club hit the deck with a crash. Shards of wood spun through the water as the timbers gave way. Tom floated just out of reach of the mace, looking for some way of getting past the knight's swinging arms. Again the mace crashed into the deck, leaving a gaping hole where it struck.

Tom darted away to avoid another swing, but his heel caught in the cracked timbers and he fell backwards through one of the jagged holes.

"No!" he yelled, bubbles flowing from his mouth as he tumbled down into the heart of the ship, landing on a dark lower deck where piles of gold and diamonds and jewels gleamed in the gloom. *So*, Tom thought dizzily as he struggled to his feet, *the legends of the lost treasure were true!*

He got ready to defend himself as the Knight plummeted down towards him. The entire wreck shook as the armoured warrior landed, ferociously swinging his mace. Tom parried the blow and leapt backwards. The mace whirled again, striking a supporting beam. The ancient timbers creaked and groaned as the beam smashed to pieces.

I need to defeat this knight quickly, Tom thought. *I mustn't give him the chance to turn into a Beast!*

Tom saw that the upper deck was caving in. The knight had destroyed

too many of the supporting beams
in his wild rampage. Timbers bent
inwards and the whole ship groaned.
Tom pushed his feet against the
deck and crashed headlong into
the knight.

The wreck shuddered as they
landed together in a heap. The hull
began to crack open and collapse.
Tom kicked off, swimming rapidly
upwards through the tumbling deck
and out of the hold. The great main
mast was leaning to one side, trailing
strands of rigging.

Tom swam high above the ship
before stopping to gaze down at
the destruction below. The knight
tried to escape from the lower part
of the ship, but the central mast
came crashing down across him. He
disappeared among the wreckage as

the mighty trunk of wood pinned
him under its great weight. Thick
dark clouds spurted from the
crumbling wreck.

Tom trod water, waiting for the
knight to emerge. The groaning and
cracking of the timbers ended as the

last pieces of the wreck settled and became still.

A blue light flashed briefly among the tangle of broken timbers. Tom stared down. *Perhaps the knight has been sent back to the Gallery of Tombs,* he thought. *Is the battle over?*

He swam down towards the heap of smashed timbers, wanting to be sure that his enemy was truly defeated. But as he drew closer, a strip of wood burst upwards, striking him in the chest. Tom was sent tumbling head over heels through the water, gasping in pain.

He stared down in dread as more timbers shot through the water. In the heart of the wreck, Tom saw something horrible emerging.

It was huge and soft and slimy. It reached up towards him with eight writing tentacles – four of them barbed with deadly blue hooks.

Surging from the wreck, a monstrous octopus-Beast oozed into view. Tom saw that it had two hideous heads and six evil blue eyes that were staring up at him with cold malice.

"Voltrex!" Tom cried.

He had been too slow – the Blue Knight had been given the chance to transform into a Beast powerful enough to crush the life from Tom's body.

The Quest had just became more deadly than ever.

CHAPTER FIVE

MONSTER FROM THE DEEP

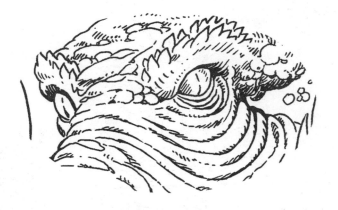

Voltrex's vast bloated body pulsated as it slithered from the wreck of *The Gorgon Voyager*. The monster's loathsome blue flesh was discoloured with green and yellow blotches, its entire body billowing and puffing out as it moved with terrifying speed from the ocean depths.

A great gaping mouth opened to

reveal a pulsing throat.

Tom didn't hesitate. *My Quest isn't over yet!* Jack-knifing his body, he shot down towards the monster with his sword drawn. His shoulder and arm ached from fighting the Blue Knight. *No pain will stop me from fighting Voltrex!* Tom vowed.

He had almost reached the swollen body of the monster when one of the tentacles whipped towards him, sweeping him effortlessly aside.

Tom tumbled over and over and crashed into the hard ridges of a reef. His side throbbed where the barbed tentacle had cut him. His blood seeped slowly into the water.

Ignoring the pain, he tried to get to his feet, but an edge of his tunic had snagged on the reef. Alarm flowed through him as he struggled to tear himself free. He could see Voltrex coming for him, the vast mouth stretching and long tentacles trailing as he surged through the water.

"Come on!" he muttered to himself as he fought his way free. "Don't give up!"

Voltrex's blue eyes shone with glee as he closed in. Green slime oozed from his throat. At the last moment, Tom ripped himself free, looking for a weapon. His hand closed on a large rock. He dragged it up and rammed it with all his strength between the razor sharp fangs.

Voltrex came to a halt. His great body pulsed above Tom, tentacles writhing through the water. The mighty jaws crunched together and the rock was crushed to pieces.

Tom felt the thick, slimy tentacles

coiling around him, tightening with hideous strength. Suckers clutched him with a grip like iron. Tom struggled as the limbs drew him in. Then he glimpsed something falling towards them through the gloomy water.

The falling object crashed into Voltrex, knocking the Beast to one side. The clinging tentacles went slack. Finding himself free of the monster's grasp, Tom squirmed clear of the open mouth. As he surged upwards, he saw that the *The Gorgon Voyager*'s anchor was lying on top of Voltrex, pinning the Beast to the seabed.

It must have knocked him senseless! Tom thought. *But how?*

Then he saw a great lithe shape close to the surface of the ocean.

A long scaly tail swept through the water.

"Sepron!" Tom cried. The Good Beast must have picked the anchor up from the seabed and dropped it onto Voltrex!

Touching Torgor's ruby that was attached to his belt, Tom swam upwards, all weariness forgotten. He knew the red jewel would allow him to communicate with Sepron. He hoped Elenna and the half-drowned woman had got safely to the shore in the terrible storm.

"Thank you, my friend," he called, coming up under the Good Beast. Guilt and dismay filled Tom as he saw a ragged wound that ran along the Sea Serpent's sinuous body. "You were injured in your battle with Voltrex," he cried. "And you still

came back to help me!"

Sepron let out a welcoming roar, obviously glad to see him.

Tom trod water, staring down to the disgusting heap of bulging flesh and slithery tentacles. It might be only moments before Voltrex came to his senses and attacked again!

Even as this thought rushed through his mind, Tom could hear a dreadful, cruel voice in his head. *Our battle is not over!* it murmured. *You cannot defeat me!*

Tom was certain that the Beast was speaking in his head somehow. Things were even more urgent than he had feared. "I have to get those tokens I left on the shore," he said to himself. "I was such a fool to leave them behind!"

"I have an idea!" he called to the Serpent. He dived down, grasping the anchor chain in both hands. Sepron joined him and together they wrapped it around Voltrex's limp tentacles. Tom knew the chain wouldn't hold the monster forever, but it might keep Voltrex from attacking until he could get back to the shore. There he could retrieve one of the magical tokens from Storm's saddlebag. Then he'd have a chance to defeat Malvel's Beast once and for all.

Tom swam alongside the Good Beast. "Sepron – quickly," he called. "Tow me to the shore."

Sepron slid alongside Tom so that he was able to get a grip on one of the Sea Serpent's fins. With a flick of his long body, the Good Beast sped to the surface.

The storm was still raging and it was all Tom could do to cling to Sepron's side as they ploughed through the crashing waves. Through salty spray and chopping seas, Tom saw that they were almost at the shore.

"You've done enough," he called to the Beast. "I'll swim the rest of the way – go to safety now! Let your wound heal!"

Sepron turned and stared at Tom with his luminous eyes. Then he flicked his long tail and slipped away, leaving Tom to paddle the short distance to land.

The waves pounded the sands all along the beach, so it wasn't easy for Tom to keep his head above water. He could see Storm galloping up and down the shoreline in panic. Close by, Elenna and Silver were at the side of the half-drowned woman. Then, as Tom was lifted by a huge rolling wave, he saw a fearsome sight.

A great dark shape was hurtling down the beach towards Elenna and Silver. Tom made out striped furry flanks and flashing white teeth.

"Elenna, watch out!" Tom shouted above the thunder. "A Varkule is coming for you!"

CHAPTER SIX

DOUBLE THE DANGER

Tom lost sight of the shoreline as he was sucked between two waves. He fought to swim ashore before the ferocious Varkule attacked his friends. He should have remembered that each of the cursed Knights of Forton was accompanied by one of the hyena-like monsters.

A wave crest lifted him again,

and Tom caught a glimpse of Silver and the Varkule doing battle in the sand. He heaved himself towards the shallows, hoping that he could reach his friends in time.

Finally Tom felt firm sand under his feet. He struggled to stand up in the rushing surf, his sword in his fist, the shield hanging heavily on his back, the ocean dragging at his legs.

"I'm coming!" he yelled above the noise of the storm. "Hold on!"

Storm was running through the surf, his eyes rolling in panic. But Tom had no time to worry about the stallion – not with a Varkule on the loose.

Two more steps and Tom would be out of the water. He brandished his sword. Elenna had an arrow to her bow, but she was having difficulty aiming as the wolf and the Varkule lunged and darted around each other on the beach.

Something slithered around Tom's legs, dragging him backwards and off his feet. He stared in fear and revulsion as a suckered tentacle wrapped itself more tightly around his chest and waist, squeezing the breath from his lungs.

He seemed to hear Voltrex's evil voice in his head again. *You are mine now!* it said. *You will die slowly.*

"Not while there's blood in my veins!" Tom howled as he brought his sword down with all his strength onto the throbbing limb. The tip of the tentacle jerked as yellowish blood spurted from the wound. Twice more Tom hacked at the tentacle, until he had severed it completely.

The end slipped away from and lay twitching in the water, while the stump recoiled, spraying more of the sickening yellow gore as it lashed to and fro. A furious roar rumbled from under the waves as Tom sprang to his feet and leapt out of the water.

He glanced back – the ocean surface was seething as Voltrex thrashed in pain and rage. In the distance, Tom saw a humped shape speeding closer, leaving a white wake in the water. Sepron was returning!

Tom ran up the beach, every limb heavy and aching from his battle, but prepared to fight to his last breath to save his friends.

Silver was rolling in the sand where the snarling Varkule had tossed him with its tusks. The Varkule turned and hurtled towards Elenna. She loosed her arrow, but it skimmed off the bristling fur along the creature's spine. She turned and looked at Tom. "Am I glad to see you!" she gasped, falling back from the Varkule and fumbling for another arrow.

With a fearsome roar, the Varkule leapt at her, its tusks aimed for her throat as thick drool spun from its open mouth.

But Silver had got to his feet, and he flung himself at their enemy, striking the Varkule in mid-air and sending him crashing into the sand. The wolf closed his jaws on the Varkule's leg, snarling and shaking his head as his fangs dug deep.

"Well done, Silver!" shouted Tom, racing up the beach.

Elenna slipped another arrow to

her bow and loosed. The arrow sank into the Varkule's side – the creature arched its neck, its legs kicking as it howled in agony. A moment later its head dropped and it stopped moving. Silver sniffed at it before giving a triumphant howl.

The Varkule was dead.

Tom turned back to the ocean, where Storm was stamping in the shallows. Now the danger of the Varkule was gone, he needed to get his stallion out of the water so he could retrieve the tokens. A fearsome sight stopped Tom in his tracks.

The ocean boiled as Sepron and Voltrex battled together in the raging storm. Sepron's head was darting this way and that on his long neck, his teeth bared as he tried to bite through the huge octopus's writhing tentacles.

But Voltrex's bulging body surged through the waves, fangs gnashing at Sepron's hide, tentacles whirling in the air and the barbs slicing at the Serpent's scales.

"I have to help him!" Tom gasped.

He spun around, seeing Storm galloping through the surf. "Here, boy!" he shouted. "I need you!"

The horse turned its head at the sound of Tom's voice. Whinnying, he galloped through the waves to where Tom was standing. Elenna and Silver were also running down to the shoreline, Elenna staring in horror at the mighty battle taking place out on the ocean.

"What can we do?" she asked.

Tom reached into the bag attached to Storm's saddle, feeling for the tokens that Aduro had given them. His fingers tingled as they closed around the miniature harpoon. *This has to be the right token to use against Voltrex, he thought.* "Go back to the shore!" Tom called to the horse.

Gripping the harpoon in his fist, Tom turned to the ocean. He gave a cry of dismay as he saw Voltrex's tentacles coiling around Sepron's body in a deadly embrace. The Sea Serpent writhed as he was lifted from the water and flung towards the shore.

Sepron crashed into the sand, his body twitching as he lay gasping on his side. A wailing moan came from the Serpent's throat as his gills opened and closed weakly in the air. He could only survive for a few precious moments out of the water. "No!" Tom cried in despair.

Was he about to see a Good Beast perish?

CHAPTER SEVEN
NEAR TO DEATH

"Elenna!" Tom called above the lashing of the rain, "I'll deal with Voltrex. Try and roll Sepron back into the ocean!"

Tom sprinted back to the water's edge while Elenna and Silver heaved against Sepron's long, scaly body with all their strength trying to push him back down the beach.

The monstrous octopus had dived

beneath the surface, leaving a churning whirlpool in his wake.

"Dive as deep as you like!" Tom cried. "I'll find you – and I'll make sure you never do any more harm!" He waded into the water, clutching the small harpoon in one hand. He knew his sword would be useless against such an evil foe.

Just before diving into the waves, he glanced at the harpoon.

What does Aduro expect me to do with this? he wondered.

Up until now in this Quest, the magical tokens given to him by the Good Wizard had been effective against the Evil Beasts he had faced. He had to trust that this small weapon would work too.

As soon as a drop of seawater hit the harpoon, it began to tingle and

grow in his hand. It thickened and
lengthened until it was as long as
a javelin. Tom gave a grim smile –
now he had a formidable weapon.
"I should never have doubted you,
Aduro," he muttered.

Tom dived into the water, swimming along under the fury of the storm-driven waves, following the seabed as it dipped away into darkness. His eyes searched for Voltrex.

But as he swam deeper, he began to feel a pain in his chest. He could still breathe, but it was becoming harder. Struggling to draw enough breath, he turned his shield and saw that Sepron's tooth was now brown and shrivelled.

The Sea Serpent must be very near to death, he thought. And once the Good Beast died, his tooth would no longer protect Tom from drowning.

Gasping, Tom struck for the surface. It felt as if an iron band was tightening around his chest. He needed air!

He broke the surface, gulping in great lungfuls of air as the rain beat down on him. The ocean was too rough for him to be able to see the shore, but he knew that Elenna would be doing everything she could to get Sepron back into the water.

"And I'll do everything I can to defeat Voltrex," Tom said to himself.

Taking a final gulp of air, Tom dived again. Kicking fiercely, he sped into the depths, the harpoon ready as he hunted for the Beast.

Tom saw a pale blue tentacle squirming through the water beneath him. He doubled his efforts, shooting downwards towards Voltrex. The bulk of the hideous monster came into view. Voltrex's tentacles flailed and the half-severed one trailed yellow blood.

Tom was directly above the vile two-headed Beast, his legs churning the water as he plunged downwards. He aimed the harpoon at the spot between the two pulsating heads. One clean strike and it would all be over.

Six evil eyes turned towards him. The monster swelled as if drawing a deep breath, then shot like an arrow towards Tom, its mouth open in a bubbling roar of fury.

The tentacles swarmed upwards and the barbed hooks whipped through the water. Tom angled his body this way and that to avoid the lashing limbs. He knocked one of the arms aside with the harpoon, but for every one he struck, more thrashed around him. Whatever he did, the tentacles twisted and thrashed, their slimy tips

eager to grasp his body and tear it
to pieces.

*How can I get close enough to strike
the Evil Beast?* he thought. Already
his lungs were straining from lack of
air, and the effort of swerving and

dodging and stabbing at the tentacles with his harpoon was draining him of energy.

A barbed hook came snaking towards him. He thrust the harpoon at it and it slithered away. But another tentacle-tip snatched at the harpoon and wrenched it from Tom's hands. He gave a gasp of dismay as he saw the harpoon spiralling downwards.

Tom drew his sword instead and swung at the lashing tentacles. His head throbbed with the lack of air and he felt sluggish and dizzy.

Twisting around, he kicked for the surface again. He needed a breath of air before trying to retrieve the harpoon. His head had just broken the waves when the water churned

and seethed around him. Tom saw
a blue barb gleaming as a tentacle
came whipping down towards him
with deadly speed.

CHAPTER EIGHT

TENTACLE ATTACK!

Tom dived under the surface and felt the tip of the barb graze across his legs. He could only hope that the air in his lungs and the remaining power in Sepron's tooth would be enough to keep him alive till he found the harpoon.

Gritting his teeth, Tom fought for more speed as he raced through the shadowy water. His lungs ached and

his limbs felt as heavy as lead. The
air was running out in his chest and
Sepron's tooth was failing. If he did
not find the harpoon quickly, all
would be lost.

Something glinted below him.
The mainmast of *The Gorgon Voyager*
was jutting up at an angle from the
seabed – and a long silvery object was
sticking out from the rigging near the
top.

The harpoon! he realised. *It got caught
in the ship's crow's nest!*

He swam closer, taking shallow breaths while there was still a flicker of power left in Sepron's tooth. But his head was spinning and he was finding it hard to focus.

A deep shadow passed over him. Voltrex was plunging down towards him, his wicked teeth glimmering like knives.

Tom grabbed the harpoon in both hands, twisting in the water and looking up to see Voltrex's cavernous mouth above him, so wide and so huge that Tom could see right down the Beast's throat.

Tom steadied himself in the water, fighting the horror and fear as well as the growing dizziness that threatened to overwhelm him. The monster's six blue eyes burned with a terrible rage and hunger. Tom drew back his arm, gripping the harpoon, aiming it between the bulging heads of the giant octopus.

Now was his final chance. If he didn't strike quickly, he'd be eaten alive. He stared up, his arm and shoulder aching as he held the harpoon ready. He fought to gulp in more air, but it seemed to make no difference to the throbbing in his head. The power in Sepron's tooth was almost gone.

Tom drew his arm back for the throw, then flung the harpoon with all his failing strength, just as one of Voltrex's tentacles struck him across the chest. He fell back into the basket of the crow's nest.

Dizzy and in pain, Tom saw the harpoon fly straight and true into the Evil Beast's gaping mouth. It struck

deep into the roof of Voltrex's maw.

The Beast writhed in agony as the harpoon sank into its soft, unprotected flesh. It jerked in the water, pushing up with its tentacles, its whole body shuddering.

The injured monster thrashed wildly with its tentacles, its body in spasms. Slowly the movements ceased and the great Beast sank down onto the wreck of *The Gorgon Voyager*. Voltrex twitched and quivered among the ruins of the old ship.

Tom drew shallow breaths, watching from the crow's nest as the defeated monster lay there on its side, quivering in his death-throes. But then it gave a final jerk and Tom's ears were filled with a mighty, booming crack, like deep thunder.

Voltrex was gone! Lying in its place was the knight in the blue armour.

Another of Malvel's Evil Beasts had been beaten – but Tom had no time to enjoy his victory. Sepron was still in peril.

Bubbles began to appear around the Blue Knight. Tom stared down at him in alarm. Was this some new danger?

The bubbles churned and foamed, so that Tom could no longer see the armoured shape. They whirled faster and faster in the water until Tom had to cling to the crow's nest to avoid being sucked down.

Then, with a sudden burst, the bubbles stopped spinning and went spiraling up towards the surface.

The knight had vanished. Tom stared at the empty place where the blue figure had been lying. *Aduro must have sent him back to the Gallery of Tombs*, he thought.

Tom pushed himself off from the crow's nest and swam as quickly as he was able for the surface. His lungs were burning now, and he dared not try to draw any more breaths under the water.

Dark spots revolved in front of his eyes. He felt like he was swimming through quicksand rather than the waters of the Western Ocean.

With his last ounce of strength, he forced his head above water. He sucked in fresh air – never had he been so close to death!

The storm was still raging as Tom struck for the shore. He ignored the lash of the rain as he swam. He had to get to Sepron before it was too late.

He reached the shallows, but as he tried to stand up in the waist-deep surf, he felt something snatch hold of his foot, tipping him forwards into the water. He was dragged backwards, gasping and gulping for air.

What now? he wondered.

He twisted under the water and saw a scaly creature grinning malevolently at him. It let out a laugh, its webbed hand pulling at his ankle.

Tom drew his sword – there was something horribly familiar about the creature's mocking laughter.

CHAPTER NINE

FIGHT FOR LIFE

"Malvel!" Tom knew that cruel laugh only too well! The Evil Wizard had somehow conjured this hideous sea creature. Tom slashed at the thing with his sword. The webbed hand released his ankle and the monster twisted around and swam away with another cackle of laughter.

"All your efforts will be in vain!" croaked the creature. "The Good

Beast will die horribly!"

Tom chased after the scaly creature,
but it went slithering along the
seabed, swifter than the fastest eel,
kicking up a cloud of sand in its wake.
Blinded by the murk, Tom rose to
the surface to take a breath.

He dived down again – but the
slithering creature was gone.

He came up for air, trembling with frustration. The creature had been created to taunt him. It must have taken a huge amount of power for Malvel to bring it to life. The Evil Wizard must almost be strong enough to break through into Avantia!

The sound of Silver barking sent Tom floundering shoreward again. He ran out of the ocean, still weakened by his ordeal. His three companions were all battling to help the stranded Sea Serpent. Elenna was pushing Sepron with all her might, but she was red-faced and looked exhausted by the effort. Silver and Storm were doing what they could, Silver butting his shoulders up against the Good Beast's body and even Storm was nudging him with his lowered head.

The woman they had rescued from

drowning had woken up and was
doing her part in the rescue, running
up and down the beach with a large
shell, filling it with water and pouring
it over Sepron's weakly flapping gills.

Tom could see by the impressions
in the sand that they had managed
to push Sepron closer to the sea –
but in doing so they had built up a

high mound of sand between Sepron and the white surf. Although the Serpent's long body was moving a little with every push, the heaped sand was making their task harder and harder.

"We have to get rid of the sand!" Tom cried, dismayed by the way the Sea Serpent's head lay so limply, the mouth hanging open, the eyes glazed and half-closed. *He's near to death*, Tom realised, his heart sinking.

Sheathing his sword, Tom used his shield to dig into the mound of sand, flinging it away, working with every sinew of his aching body. Silver leapt over Sepron's body and joined Tom, working furiously with all four paws, gouging holes in the sand mound and kicking it away. Elenna and the woman added their strength to the task, the woman using the shell to dig, Elenna on her knees, scrabbling with both hands.

"We're too late!" moaned Elenna, almost weeping in her misery. "He's already dead!"

"No!" gasped Tom. "There's still a flicker of life! We must work harder!"

Storm was doing what he could by kicking the sand away with his back legs.

Tom stood up, his back aching from the strain, the sweat pouring into his eyes. The mound of sand was all but gone. "That's it!" he called. "Now we have to push for Sepron's life!"

They raced around the other side of Sepron and heaved at his sagging body. For a dreadful moment Tom doubted they had the strength left to move him. His arms burned and he gritted his teeth. "Keep pushing!" he hissed.

Suddenly the Sea Serpent rolled over in the sand, into the shallow surf. Seawater washed around him.

"Deeper!" Tom shouted. "We must get him right under the water!"

It was a mighty effort, the two animals and the three humans using the last of their strength to try and save the Good Beast.

Sepron rolled again, moving deeper into the frothing and splashing water. Waves broke against his green scaly body and white foam flew.

With one final push, the Good Beast slipped under the water and the waves of the Western Ocean rolled over him.

Gasping for breath, Tom, Elenna and the woman stood knee-deep in the churning water, waiting anxiously for the creature to wake up.

Silver stood close to Elenna, his wet hair plastered flat onto his body, his eyes on the unmoving Beast. Storm butted his head against Tom's shoulder, as though trying to ask whether Sepron would be all right.

"Come on, Sepron," Tom whispered. "You can do it!" His thundering heart filled with pain and loss. Sepron didn't stir at all.

"Why isn't he moving?" cried Elenna, her hands up to her face. "Oh, no! We took too long!"

Tom waded deeper and ducked his head under the waves. He tried to breathe in the water, but it choked him and he had to bob to the surface to take in some air. Sepron's tooth had failed.

He's dead! Tom thought. *I've failed!* He swam along the Serpent's body to his great fronded head. The Beast's gills were not moving at all. Even the Good Beast's scales had lost their usual sheen and Tom saw that Sepron's eyes were closed.

Tom's heart felt heavy in his chest as he gave Sepron's snout a farewell touch and then turned away, swimming into the shallows.

"Is he...?" asked Elenna as Tom waded towards the shore.

Tom's throat was clogged with grief. He couldn't speak. He could only shake his head.

Tears ran down Elenna's face and Silver let out a mournful howl.

Tom had almost made it to the beach when something struck his legs hard from behind, tipping him into the water.

Had Malvel returned again?

CHAPTER TEN

FEAR IN THE DAWN

The water closed over Tom's head
as he fell. He gasped for breath,
forgetting for a moment that Sepron's
tooth could no longer protect him
from drowning.

But his lungs filled with air!

He twisted around in the water and
came almost face to face with the Sea
Serpent. Sepron's eyes were wide
open, bright with renewed life, and

his gills moved vigorously.

The Good Beast's tail flicked playfully at Tom, rolling him over as he began to laugh. It must have been a knock from Sepron's tail that had tipped him off his feet.

"You're alive!" Tom shouted, grinning from ear to ear.

Sepron let out a tremendous roar, his eyes shining as his scales rippled with every colour of the rainbow.

"But you're still wounded," Tom said, noticing again the cruel red gash in Sepron's scales. "Wait here – I can heal you."

Tom bobbed to the surface, smiling. "Tom!" gasped Elenna, her voice full of anxiety. "What's happened?"

"Sepron is alive!" he shouted. "Look!" At that moment, the Serpent's head erupted from the

waves and the Sea Serpent let out
another friendly roar.

"That's wonderful," cried Elenna.
Silver howled for joy and Storm
reared up in the surf and let out a
deafening neigh. Even the woman
clapped her hands together and
laughed, although she also looked
quite surprised at the sight of the
huge Beast.

Tom swam alongside Sepron, taking Epos the Flame Bird's healing talon from his shield. "Keep still, Sepron!" Tom called as he gently pressed the talon along the wound. The painful-looking gash closed at the talon's magical touch.

"Thank you for your help!" Tom shouted as Sepron sped out into deeper water and cavorted in the waves, his body sliding through the waves in thick winding coils.

With a final roar, the Sea Serpent turned his head towards the horizon and sped away, heading for his underwater home.

Tom waded to the shore.

"The storm has finally ended," Elenna said, gazing into the east. "And look – the sun is coming out!"

In the eastern sky the clouds were

ragged and broken, and a pearly light was swiftly coming out.

Worn out by their efforts, Tom and Elenna sat in the sand, bathed in the last of the lightly falling rain. The woman came and knelt in front of them.

"I haven't had the time to thank you for rescuing me," she said.

"You're welcome," said Tom.

"How did you come to be out in the ocean?" Elenna asked.

"My name is Arianna," the woman explained while Silver and Storm came and stood close by. "I'm an artist. I was drawing on the beach." She smiled. "A favourite subject of mine – *The Gorgon Voyager.*" She shuddered. "But a knight in blue armour came out of the water and attacked me."

Tom drew the crumpled piece of
parchment from his tunic, smoothing
it out and showing it to her. "This
knight?" he asked.

Arianna nodded. "I just had time to
draw that before he caught hold of
me and dragged me into the ocean."
She took the picture from Tom
and tore it to shreds. "I don't want
to be reminded of him!" she said,

scattering the pieces. But then a smile widened on her face. "But something wonderful came of it – when the knight took me under the waves, I saw a brief glimpse of *The Gorgon Voyager* on the seabed." She sighed. "Then he released me and I drifted helplessly, wrapped in seaweed, until you found me."

"The legend is true, then?" said Elenna. "There really is a lost treasure ship down there?"

"There is," admitted Tom. "And I saw more of it than I would have liked. But it's been smashed to pieces now."

"You fought the knight on the shipwreck?" asked Elenna.

Tom nodded, and started to tell them all that had happened under the waves.

As he spoke, the rising sun chased the last of the clouds away over the ocean and their wet clothes began to dry in the welcome warmth.

Tom shook his head. "It was the hardest fight yet," he said. "With each new knight, the Quest is getting more difficult." He looked at his companion. "This time I almost lost one of the Good Beasts."

Elenna looked anxiously at him. "But we won, Tom," she said. "And we can't stop now. We won't let Malvel beat us, will we?"

Tom got to his feet, stroking Storm's mane as he gazed out over the Western Ocean. The last few clouds glowed with a silvery sheen in the sunlight. Where the distant rain still fell, a rainbow glowed over the water.

"I will rid Avantia of the final two

Knights of Forton," Tom said. "And then I'll face Malvel." He looked at Elenna, his face grim. "I have a feeling that this will be our final battle, Elenna," he said. "This time, the fight will not be over until one of us is defeated for good!"

Join Tom on the next stage
of the Beast Quest when he meets

TECTON
THE ARMOURED
GIANT

Win an exclusive
Beast Quest T-shirt and goody bag!

In every Beast Quest book the Beast Quest logo is hidden in one of the pictures. Find the logos in books 55 to 60 and make a note of which pages they appear on. Write the six page numbers on a postcard and send it in to us.
Each month we will draw one winner to receive a Beast Quest T-shirt and goody bag.

THE BEAST QUEST COMPETITION:
THE MASTER OF THE BEASTS
Orchard Books
338 Euston Road, London NW1 3BH
Australian readers should email:
childrens.books@hachette.com.au

New Zealand readers should write to:
Beast Quest Competition
4 Whetu Place, Mairangi Bay, Auckland, NZ
or email: childrensbooks@hachette.co.nz

Only one entry per child.
Final draw: 4 March 2013

You can also enter this competition
via the Beast Quest website: www.beastquest.co.uk

Join the Quest,
Join the Tribe

www.beastquest.co.uk

Have you checked out the Beast Quest website? It's the place to go for games, downloads, activities, sneak previews and lots of fun!

You can read all about your favourite Beasts, download free screensavers and desktop wallpapers for your computer, and even challenge your friends to a Beast Tournament.

Sign up to the newsletter at www.beastquest.co.uk to receive exclusive extra content and the opportunity to enter special members-only competitions. We'll send you up-to-date info on all the Beast Quest books, including the next exciting series which features six brand-new Beasts!